The Case of the Feathered Mask

For Thea
—H.W.

For Dinah and John, with love and thanks
—M.L.

Text copyright © 2014 by Holly Webb
Illustrations copyright © 2014 by Marion Lindsay

First published in Great Britain in 2014 by Stripes Publishing, an imprint of Little Tiger Press.

All rights reserved. For information about permission to reproduce selections from this book, write to trade.permissions@hmhco.com or to Permissions, Houghton Mifflin Harcourt Publishing Company, 3 Park Avenue, 19th Floor, New York, New York 10016.

www.hmhco.com

Text set in ITC Garamond

The Library of Congress has cataloged the hardcover edition as follows:
Webb, Holly.
The case of the feathered mask/written by Holly Webb;
illustrated by Marion Lindsay.
p. cm.—(The mysteries of Maisie Hitchens)
Summary: Junior sleuth Maisie Hitchens, who lives in her grandmother's boarding house in Victorian London, investigates the theft of a rare and valuable tribal mask from the Amazonian rainforest.
[1. Mystery and detective stories—Fiction. 2. Boardinghouses—Fiction. 3. Masks—Fiction. 4. London (England)—History—19th century—Fiction. 5. Great Britain—History—Victoria, 1837–1901—Fiction.]
I. Lindsay, Marion, illustrator. II. Title.
PZ7.W368Caj 2016
[Fic]—dc23
2014048388

ISBN: 978-0-544-61993-7 hardcover
ISBN: 978-0-544-94884-6 paperback

Manufactured in the United States of America
DOC 10 9 8 7 6 5 4 3 2 1

4500644154

THE MYSTERIES OF
MAISIE HITCHINS

The Case of the Feathered Mask

BOOK 4

written by
Holly Webb

illustrated by
Marion Lindsay

Houghton Mifflin Harcourt | Boston New York

31 Albion Street, London

Attic:

Maisie's grandmother and Sally the maid

Third floor:

Miss Lane's rooms

Second floor:

Madame Lorimer's rooms

First floor:

Professor Tobin's rooms

Ground floor:

Entrance hall, sitting room, and dining room

Basement:

Maisie's room, kitchen, and yard entrance

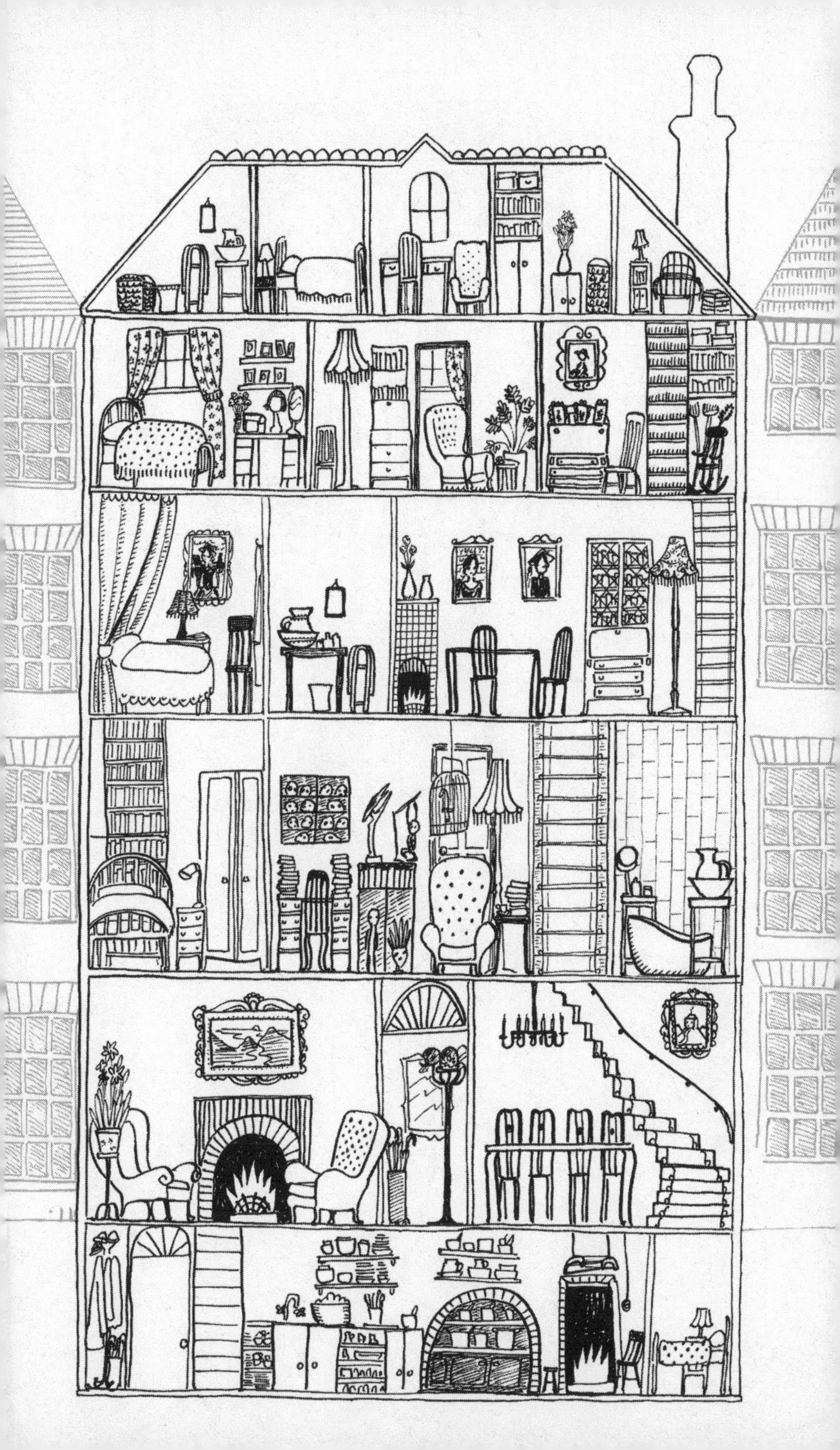

"But I don't see why you want to give all these things away, Professor."

Maisie stood in the middle of Professor Tobin's rooms and gazed at the boxes stacked up around her. Wooden packing cases were shedding straw all over the carpet, which Maisie would have to sweep. But she didn't mind—she was very fond of the professor and quite often lingered over the dusting in his rooms so he could tell her stories about his expeditions.

In return, Maisie would tell him all about the latest mysteries she'd solved. Like how she had discovered that the old lady who lived at the end of the road had a secret addiction to toffee bonbons.

"Won't you miss all your things?" Maisie asked. She lifted up a glass case containing tiny stuffed birds perched on a branch and carefully tucked it into one of the boxes. She would miss the amazing objects they were packing away, even if the professor wouldn't. Although it would be nice not to have so many glass cases to polish.

"Oh, of course, of course." Professor Tobin nodded as he patted a wooden carving lovingly. "But I'm running out of room, Maisie. No more wall space." Then he beamed at her. "A museum is the best place for them. Most of the animal specimens will go to the new Natural History Museum, in Kensington, now that it's finally finished. And the masks and carvings to the British Museum. There's to be a Tobin Room," he added, smiling shyly. "Besides, if I give most of my collection to the museum, I shall simply have to go on another expedition and find some more artifacts, won't I?"

"I suppose so," Maisie agreed sadly. She hated the idea of the professor leaving. His last expedition, which he'd returned from several months before, had been all across South America, and he had told her that he'd been away for years.

"I won't be off for a while, Maisie—don't worry. I haven't finished my book yet. And when I do go away, I shall keep my rooms here in your grandmother's house, and you must promise to look after Jasper for me."

Maisie sighed quietly. Jasper was the professor's parrot, and it was one of her jobs to clean his cage and fill his bowls with water and seed. Maisie had always thought that parrots were intelligent, but Jasper most definitely wasn't. He was very handsome, with beautiful bright red feathers, but he was certainly a birdbrain. He had a terrible tendency to sit in his water bowl and tip it over, and then shiver pathetically in the corner of his cage until someone came and dried him. He didn't talk much, either. He would look hopefully at anyone who came into the room, and squawk, "Bikkit?" That was about it, though.

Maisie's gran couldn't stand the parrot, but the professor was her best lodger. His rooms were the most expensive in the boarding house. Plus, he always paid his rent on time. So she pretended not to notice Jasper at all.

"Yes, I'll look after him," Maisie said. She glanced over at the big cage, which hung from a stand by the window—the professor was convinced that Jasper liked to look out. "Oh, he's upside down," she said in surprise, peering at the parrot, who was clinging to the top of his cage with his knobby gray claws.

"Don't tell him! Oh, too late." Professor

Tobin flinched as Jasper panicked, let go, and crashed into his food bowl, spraying sunflower seeds everywhere.

"I'll fetch the broom," Maisie sighed.

While Maisie swept up the mess, she told the professor about her morning's work. She had actually been paid for her detecting, for once—a whole shilling. Mr. Lacey, father of Maisie's best friend, Alice, had employed her to investigate Alice's new governess. Mr. Lacey had wanted to make sure the new governess was nicer than Miss Sidebotham, who had left her post after a disastrous stay in the country with Alice and Maisie.

Maisie had lurked in the hallway, with a duster, to look at the candidates as they came to be interviewed. "Mr. Lacey just wanted to know what I thought about them, you see. He said I've got a good eye," she added proudly. "It wasn't easy, though. I mean, what do I know about governesses? I did tell him not to even think about the one with the fox-fur collar on her coat, because someone who could walk about with a beady-eyed dead fox around her neck all the time absolutely has to be horrible, don't you think?" she asked the professor.

He nodded solemnly. "They'd have to be."

Of course, the job was made more complicated because Maisie was secretly working for Alice at the same time (although Alice was only paying her in toffee). She wanted to be sure that none of the possible new governesses would try to marry her father. Alice had always claimed that Miss Sidebotham was trying to do exactly that.

It was unfortunate that Mr. Lacey was kind, rich, hardworking, and in possession of a most attractive and curly mustache. Maisie had a dreadful feeling that even the most hard-hearted governess would fall in love with him. Maisie had suggested to Alice that perhaps she should go to school instead of having a governess. Not the ordinary school that Maisie had been to before she left to work in Gran's boarding house, of course, but a smart establishment for young ladies. Alice rather liked the idea, but then she had realized she would have to leave her darling white cats behind.

"So Alice said she'd just have to take her chances with a new governess instead, you see. There!" Maisie glared at Jasper as she swept the last of the sunflower seeds into her dustpan. "Don't do it again, you silly creature!"

"I'll be glad when those dratted stuffed animals are all gone," Gran snapped. "You spend half your time up there dusting them, and now on top of that we've got sightseers hanging around outside!" She peered around the heavy velvet curtains and sniffed crossly. "I never thought I'd live to see the day—my respectable boarding house being written up in the newspapers."

Maisie leaned around her gran to look through the window of the sitting room. Hardly anyone used the little front room, but Gran insisted on keeping it dusted and polished till all the furniture shone. It was where she interviewed new lodgers and important visitors—as she said, she could hardly talk to them in the kitchen, which was where she and Maisie and Sally the maid spent most of their time.

"I think it's quite exciting," Maisie said as she watched a young man in a smart overcoat point up at the rooms on the first floor. He could probably see Jasper, she decided. That was if Jasper hadn't fallen off his perch again. "And they aren't saying anything bad, Gran. Just that the famous Professor Tobin lives here. And he's giving all his specimens to the museums."

"And now there's straw everywhere from his grubby packing cases," Gran sighed. "Those nasty flea-bitten things can't go too soon, as far as I'm concerned."

Maisie decided not to tell Gran that the professor was only giving his collection away so that he could go and gather more strange objects. It would just upset her. "Oooh, who's that?" she asked, pointing at a tall, thin young man in a very well brushed silk top hat and shiny spats who was parading down the street.

"He might not be calling here," Gran said hopefully. "Oh, but he is! He's knocking! Run and fetch me a clean apron, Maisie, for goodness' sake. And don't let that dog out! He looks like the sort of gentleman that can't abide dog hairs on his trousers!"

Maisie galloped down the stairs, making sure to shut Eddie in the kitchen. Gran liked Eddie more than she let on, but the little dog still managed to get himself into trouble all the time.

Gran answered the door in her best black silk apron, and the man bowed at her, in a rather smarmy sort of way.

"Good afternoon, madam. Gerald Danvers."

Gran stared at him. She hadn't a clue who he was, and neither had Maisie, who was lurking at the bottom of the stairs to see what was happening.

"Er, yes?"

"Gerald Danvers. From the British Museum. Professor Tobin is expecting me." The young man looked rather annoyed —his thin lips went even thinner—and he looked down his nose at Maisie's gran. Maisie decided she definitely didn't like him. She wasn't sure the British Museum deserved the professor's collection if they were all as snobbish as this man was.

Still, Gran wasn't easily quashed, especially when she had her best apron on. "Indeed?" she said icily. "Professor Tobin didn't mention that he was expecting a visitor."

"Must I really be kept waiting on the doorstep, my good woman?" Mr. Danvers sniffed, and Maisie saw Gran's ears turn red. She hated it when people were rude.

"We can't be too careful, can we? Maisie, run upstairs and see if the professor is at home to Mr . . . Denby, did you say your name was?"

"Danvers!"

"Oh yes. Mr. Dinbers, Maisie."

Maisie hurried up to the professor's rooms and stuck her head around the door. "Professor, there's a gent here from the British Museum. Shall I bring him up?"

"Oh, dash it, it'll be that Danvers fellow. Come to examine the masks again. Can't wait to get his grubby little paws on them." The professor looked up, red-faced. He'd been trying to wedge a wallaby into a packing case that wasn't quite wide enough, and he didn't seem to be in the mood for visitors. "I suppose you better had, Maisie, infernal bore though he is."

Maisie trotted back downstairs and led the snooty Mr. Danvers up after her, while Gran muttered crossly on her way back down to the kitchen.

"Thank you, Maisie," the professor murmured. "Could you try to clear up some of this straw? From the chairs, perhaps, so Mr. Danvers can sit down?"

Maisie bustled about, tidying up, while Mr. Danvers admired the collection.

"Amazing assortment of stuffed creatures, sir," he said, peering into the packing cases. Maisie didn't think he meant it. His nostrils were twitching, as though he thought the animals smelled. "A very fine llama here," he added, waving a limp hand.

Maisie peered into the case as she whisked past with a dustpan, and sniggered. She knew perfectly well it was a wombat in the box he was looking at—the professor had told her.

Mr. Danvers raised his eyeglass and stared at Maisie with dislike.

"Ah, yes. The—er—wombat. Easily confused, my dear fellow. Very much like a llama. Just smaller." The professor pulled out a large spotted handkerchief and buried his face in it, trying to look as though he wasn't sniggering too.

Gerald Danvers glared furiously after Maisie as she hurried away to fetch the tea, but Maisie didn't care that she'd been rude. He'd been much ruder.

Maisie and Eddie hurried back along Albion Street. The professor had sent her out to buy two pennyworth of nails to fasten up the last of the packing cases, which was good, as he'd probably give Maisie a penny for herself, too. She'd be able to buy Eddie a nice bone at the butcher's.

"Oh, look, Eddie," Maisie muttered. "Another nosy parker waiting outside. It's that newspaper article. It made it sound like the professor was keeping half the treasures of the Americas in our house. People think they're going to see great big gold statues, I suppose."

The man standing outside number 31 was quite elderly, and he was swathed in layers of scarves against the chilly March weather. His bowler hat was tipped forward over his nose, so that all Maisie could really see of him was a long, droopy mustache.

"I hope Gran hasn't noticed," Maisie told Eddie. "She hates all these people standing about. Maybe I can get rid of him." She coughed politely as she came up beside him. "May I help you, sir? I live here."

"Oh . . ." The man stared at her, and then took a step backwards, his head turning from side to side, like a trapped animal. Then he turned and hurried off down the street.

"That was easier than I thought it would

be," Maisie said, looking down at Eddie in surprise. "I wonder why he was so nervous. Perhaps he was another professor." Professor Tobin had entertained a few learned gentlemen, and as far as Maisie could tell, all professors were odd. Either they were wearing most of their breakfast, or they had their waistcoats buttoned up wrong. And they all, every single one, had eyebrows like big, furry caterpillars.

"We'd better go and take these nails upstairs," she said when the strange man had vanished around the corner. "The men from the museum are coming early tomorrow morning."

Fastening up the cases took longer than Maisie had thought it would. It seemed that as soon as the professor had one tightly nailed shut, he would suddenly remember something vitally important that should have been on a label and would have to pry all the nails out again.

Maisie suspected that actually he didn't need to undo the cases at all. It was just harder for the professor to give up his treasures than he had thought it would be. He didn't want to say goodbye.

At last the professor collapsed into his armchair, almost squashing Eddie, who had sneaked into it when neither of them was looking. "Oh dear . . ." he said wearily. "Don't worry, Maisie, I shall finish that last case tomorrow morning. All the specimens for the Natural History Museum are ready —that's good. It's only the masks and those carvings that still need to be packed." He sighed and looked up at an eerie wooden mask hanging on the wall. It was carved with dark, squarish eyes and a hooked, beaklike nose, and fringed with bright red feathers that looked remarkably like Jasper's. "You're a good girl, Maisie. You've been a great help."

Maisie looked down at him, concerned. "You do want to give them away still, don't you? You haven't changed your mind?"

"No, no . . . It's a little sad, Maisie, that's all. Some of these things I've had for many years. And some were given to me. But it's right that they should be in a museum for everyone to see. It's selfish to keep them here all to myself. I'm keeping a few smaller things, some of the things that I love. But they're a little battered, or not so rare." He waved a hand at a rather tatty-looking wooden mask with a furry trim, not nearly as smart as the red-feathered one.

Maisie nodded. Even she could see that

the man from the museum wouldn't be as excited about that.

"I shall keep this one, you see. And of course I can always go and look at the other artifacts in the museum, like everyone else . . ."

"And you *are* going to go and get more, after all," Maisie reminded him. "You need to make room."

Lugging boxes around in between all her other work had left Maisie exhausted. She crawled wearily under her blankets and felt Eddie snuggle up warmly beside her.

She must have fallen asleep at once, and it felt like only seconds later that she was dragged awake again.

"Oh, Eddie, shhh! Shhh! You'll wake the

whole house. What is it?" She could hear him dancing about in front of the door, his claws clicking on the stone floor, and then scrabbling frantically at the wood. "What is it? Didn't I put any newspaper down?" She had trained him very carefully, and he hardly ever made a mess. Maisie lit her candle and looked around, but the newspaper was there, just as it usually was. Something else was wrong. Eddie was barking—and he kept looking at her as though he couldn't understand why she wouldn't let him out.

Maisie gulped. She'd never seen him like this before. "Is someone in the house?" she whispered. "Is it a burglar?"

She got out of bed, her heart thumping. She could feel it, high up and tight in her throat. She wanted to crawl underneath her bed where no one would find her. But Gran was upstairs, and Sally, and Miss Lane, and the professor, and old Madame Lorimer, too. Detectives did not hide under beds. Her hero, the detective Gilbert Carrington, would fetch his swordstick and be off up those stairs straightaway.

Maisie didn't have a swordstick, but she picked up a large, heavy frying pan from the kitchen on her way past. Eddie had stopped barking now—he was growling instead, in an angry, breathy sort of way. He sounded as though he'd like to bite a lump out of any burglar, but he was so tiny and Maisie didn't want him to get hurt. "Heel, Eddie," she whispered comfortingly.

They came up the stairs from the kitchen into the hallway, and Maisie peered anxiously up the next flight of stairs. She couldn't hear anything—but was that a faint light coming from the professor's rooms? She held her candle up to the grandfather clock, which said four o'clock. The middle of the night. Even if the professor had decided to stay up to finish packing, surely he'd have gone to bed by now.

Maisie stepped slowly up the stairs to the first floor, wondering whether to scream and wake everyone up or try to catch the thief unawares with her frying pan. *Did the thief hear Eddie barking?* she wondered. The lodgers were used to hearing him bark every so often—they had probably just cursed him, stuck their heads under their pillows, and gone back to sleep. But the burglar didn't know that. He would be expecting the household to come searching—and he didn't know that Eddie was only little, either.

So whoever it was, he was very

determined. Maybe even desperate.

Maisie gulped and wondered if even Gilbert Carrington might go and find some help in this sort of situation. Perhaps she could find a policeman in the street? She turned to look down the stairs again, peering out of the fanlight window over the door. It was very dark.

Then there was a crash and a thudding of footsteps. Maisie gasped. The thief was coming! She grabbed determinedly at the great heavy figure that went blundering past her down the stairs. But whoever it was pushed her back, and Maisie felt herself waver on the edge of a step. She reached for the banister, but it slid away from her fingers as though it were greased, and she began to fall, bumping down the hard wooden stairs after the burglar.

"Ohhhh!" she wailed, and Eddie yelped, scrabbling down the stairs after her.

Maisie landed with a thud at the bottom, her head ringing where she'd banged it against the banister. She felt dazed and sick, and her candle had gone out. She couldn't see a thing. She could feel Eddie sniffing at her, his damp nose on her cheek as he tried to see if she was all right. Then Eddie yapped and darted away through the open front door after the intruder. Maisie watched the faint white blur disappear into the darkness, and then she leaned her aching head against the wall and closed her eyes.

"Maisie! Maisie! Wake up, dear child!"

Maisie blinked, and squinted her eyes to shut out the painful lamplight.

"Ah, you're awake. Don't worry, Mrs. Hitchins, she's coming round. Whatever happened, Maisie?" It was the professor's voice, sharp and anxious. "Did you fall down the stairs? What were you doing up at this time of night?"

"A burglar . . ." Maisie looked up at him, and saw Gran and Sally and Miss Lane all leaning over her, their faces worried.

"A burglar!" Gran gasped. "She's right, the front door's half open! My silver teapot!"

"No . . . He was in the professor's room. Oh! Where's Eddie? He went after the thief —I should have stopped him, but my head was all dizzy and I couldn't really think. Is he back? What if the burglar hurt him?"

"It's all right." Miss Lane, the actress who rented the third-floor rooms, pointed at the front steps. "There he is."

Maisie turned carefully to look. She was trying to keep her head as still as possible, to stop it hurting.

Eddie heaved himself up the front steps toward her, one paw at a time, and Maisie took in a worried breath. Usually he raced up steps, full of energy. “Eddie!” she cried. “Did he hurt you?”

“I think he’s just tired, Maisie,” the professor said, running a hand over Eddie’s back. “He’s panting.”

Eddie’s tongue was hanging out as he slumped onto the floor next to Maisie, and she patted him lovingly. “Good boy! Did you chase that burglar?”

Eddie seemed to nod, as though he understood, and then he spat out a mouthful of something reddish and slobbery onto Maisie’s nightdress.

“What on earth has that dog gone and done now?” Gran sighed. “What *is* that disgusting mess?”

“Feathers . . .” Maisie murmured, pulling out one damp feather and examining it.

“Oh, no, Professor—did the thief take

one of your stuffed birds? Or Jasper? The feathers are the same color, that bright red . . ." She stopped, trying to remember where else she had seen red feathers recently. It was hard when she felt so dizzy. She could see a face, hook-nosed and dark-eyed, somehow mixed up with the feathers. But it wasn't the thief—she hadn't really seen his face. In fact, she couldn't remember anything about him, except that he'd pushed her out of the way as if she'd weighed nothing at all. *It must have been the bang on the head that did it,* Maisie thought.

Professor Tobin leaned over and picked up another of the feathers, running it between his fingers and frowning. Then an expression of horror came over his face.

"The mask! The feathered mask!"

The professor had looked so upset that Gran had sent everyone upstairs to sit down while she made a pot of strong tea.

Now he was sitting huddled in his armchair, cocooned in his emerald green dressing gown, with his nightcap on sideways. His hands were wrapped around his teacup, and his face was pale and pouchy-looking.

"I shall have to go to the police tomorrow. That mask is one of the treasures of my collection," he explained wearily, staring at the empty spot on the wall where the mask had been. "Incredibly rare, you see. In fact, there isn't another one like it—not outside the Amazon, anyway."

"The Amazon?" Maisie breathed. "That huge river? Where they have the fish that eat people?"

"Well, yes. Though the stories of the piranha fish are very much exaggerated," the professor said reassuringly, seeing Sally and Miss Lane turn pale. "Some of them actually prefer fruit."

"So you've been to the Amazon?" Miss Lane asked him, wide-eyed. "That's where the mask came from?"

"Yes . . ." The professor sighed. "I have to admit, I can't pinpoint exactly where. I was rather lost at the time, you see. My canoe had been overturned by an enormous caiman—rather like an alligator, you know. I found myself washed up on the bank of the river, with only a small amount of my equipment and none of my companions. I later discovered that they had given me up for dead! In fact, several of my friends had raised money for a most handsome memorial plaque in the dining hall at my old university. They were quite annoyed when I turned up again."

Maisie giggled. "How did you get back home?"

"Well, I went exploring along the riverbank, and I happened to come across one of the forest-dwellers, a tribesman who was out hunting."

"Was he fierce?" Sally gasped. "I've heard some of these forest tribes use poison darts that make you fall down stiff as a board!"

"He probably would have been," the professor agreed, "except that when I saw him, he was wrapped in the coils of a giant anaconda. That's a snake," he added when everyone looked at him blankly. "And this one was twenty-two feet long—I measured it. Afterwards . . ."

"After what? What did you do?" Maisie asked excitedly. "Did you rescue the man?"

"I removed my cravat and tied it round the neck of the snake. Then I used it to pull the snake away from the man. Luckily, some of his fellow tribesmen heard me shouting and came to help. We managed to get the snake to let go, and the tribesmen cut its head off." The professor sighed regretfully.

"Didn't you want them to kill it? A monstrous snake?" Gran gave a horrified sniff.

"Well, yes. But it was such a grand creature, Mrs. Hitchins. It seemed a pity. Anyway, it turned out that Achuchi was some sort of tribal elder—a chieftain. They were very grateful to me for saving him, at any rate."

"And they gave you the mask to say thank you." Maisie nodded. "Did they show you how to get home, as well?"

"Yes, but I stayed with them for a few months, first. My leg had been injured in the fight with the anaconda, and I needed to let it heal before I could travel. I enjoyed teaching them some English as well. And they were very welcoming. Even though I did get rather sick of roasted anaconda. When eventually I was ready to leave, there was a great ceremony with the whole tribe singing and dancing, and that's when they presented me with the mask. I have a photograph, over there, on my desk."

He started to get to his feet, but Sally jumped up first and picked up the picture. Maisie had often polished the smart silver frame and looked at the figures, but she hadn't known the story behind the photograph.

The professor stood in the middle, holding the mask. On one side of him was a wrinkled little man, with a piece of fabric wrapped around his waist like a skirt. That was all he was wearing apart from a beautiful necklace that seemed to be made

of feathers and teeth. On the other side of Professor Tobin was a boy, smiling widely.

"A very successful picture, bearing in mind that I had to teach one of the boys to use the camera and then carry the photographic plate all the way back to London with me," the professor said proudly. "It was just lucky that the camera was properly packed and wrapped in oilskins before the caiman attacked."

"Who is the boy?" Maisie asked. He looked about the same age as her.

"Ah, that's Daniel. Well, I called him Daniel. He was Achuchi's grandson, and my most keen pupil in the study of English. I told him the story of Daniel in the lions' den, and he was so taken with it that he decided to adopt the name for himself." The professor smiled. "You remind me of him, Maisie. So determined. I offered to take him back to England with me, you know. So he could be educated. But he was too close to his tribe, and the forest. He couldn't imagine living anywhere else."

The professor gazed at the empty spot on the wall again. "That mask was the pride of my collection. So beautifully carved and delicately painted. I wanted other people to see it, to see the art that had gone into making it. So many people in our country talk about those who live in South America as savages, you see, when they're no such thing."

Maisie saw Sally and Miss Lane exchange doubtful glances. Hunting in forests and living on roast snake clearly sounded like savage behavior to them. But the mask had been beautiful, and eerie. She could see what the professor meant.

"We'll get it back . . ." she said, trying to sound encouraging.

The professor smiled at her, but he didn't look very hopeful. In fact, he looked downright miserable.

Gran patted his shoulder. "Go back to bed, Professor. We all should, for that matter. There's nothing to be done until the morning, after all."

The professor nodded. "You're right, of

course, Mrs. Hitchins," he said with a sigh.

Maisie gritted her teeth. The professor thought there was nothing to be done, she could tell. But she was going to do whatever it took to get the mask back for him. No one in the house had seen the thief, which meant it would be a tricky test of her detective skills. If only she could remember more about what had happened.

Halfway up the stairs, Maisie sat down and sighed. She was just where she had been in the middle of the night, but it wasn't helping her remember anything. Gran had told her to rest after her fall, but Maisie had been eager to sweep and polish the stairs, for once. She had been hoping that being there would jog her memory and she would suddenly remember what the thief had looked like. Or something he had said. Or anything.

She hadn't been able to find a single clue in the professor's rooms—just that bare space where the mask had been. The policemen who had examined the rooms earlier that morning hadn't found anything either. Maisie had lurked on the landing and listened.

She looked around again hopefully. But the stairs were just the stairs, and they looked exactly like they always did. Except that there was a scratch on the wallpaper next to where Maisie was sitting. Gran seemed more worried about that than she was about the loss of the mask, as the wallpaper was quite new. Maisie thought it must be where the thief had bumped against the wall when they collided with each other on the stairs. But the scratch wasn't telling her anything useful at all.

Maisie shook her head. Why couldn't she remember anything? It didn't help that she was so tired from getting up in the middle of the night. By the time she had gotten back to bed again it had been five o'clock, and she and Gran and Sally usually got up at six. Slowly, Maisie clambered to her feet and walked back up to the top step to begin polishing the banisters.

It seemed to take her hours to get all the way down the stairs, and now she had to polish the dratted newel post. Maisie cursed the thing whenever she had to clean it. It was full of fiddly bits that trapped the dust, and it was a beast to get shiny. She sighed as she scooped up a bit of beeswax polish on her cloth.

She was just about to wipe it over the newel post when a flash of color caught her eye. Maisie peered at the carved wood. There was a scrap of fabric caught in it. She gasped. A clue! It had to be! Gran made her polish the banisters at least twice a week —she was very particular about them, as she said the lodgers were up and down all day, dirtying them up with finger marks. The fabric definitely hadn't been there the other day—so it must belong to the thief, surely.

Maisie stared at it for a second, wide-eyed, and then raced back up the stairs and up the next two flights, to Miss Lane's rooms. She knocked loudly and there was a moan from inside.

"Who on earth is that? It's the middle of the night!"

"Sorry! It's me, Maisie! Miss Lane, do you have some tweezers I could borrow? And it's actually ten in the morning."

"Ten! Exactly! That *is* the middle of the night! Yes, Maisie, if you can find them, you can borrow them. But only if you're completely silent so I can go back to sleep."

Maisie crept inside the sitting room and peeped around the door into the actress's bedroom. Miss Lane wriggled further under her pretty satin coverlet, so that Maisie

could see only her curling papers as she
tiptoed across to the mirrored dressing table.

Ah, there were the tweezers, just as she'd thought. She seized them and darted away, hopping over discarded shawls, piles of play scripts, and abandoned cups of tea. She cleaned Miss Lane's rooms twice a week, but they were still always messy.

Back at the bottom of the stairs, Maisie used the tweezers to pull the scrap of fabric away from the carved wood without tearing it. It was tiny, no bigger than a penny, and very fine. Maisie frowned. It was almost like summer dress fabric. Not like something a man would wear. It was patterned, she thought, although it was hard to tell from such a small piece. Yellow, with red shapes, perhaps? It wasn't really like anything she'd seen before.

Maisie wrapped it up carefully in a leaf of paper that she tore from the little notebook she kept in her apron pocket. She would give it to the professor later, and he could pass it on to the police. But she would keep it to herself, just for a little while. She was the only witness, after all. It might jog her memory.

Could it have been a woman who had stolen the mask and barged into her on the stairs? Whoever it was must have been thrown off-balance and then bumped into the newel post at the bottom and caught her skirt, or the hem of her coat . . . No. Maisie eyed the newel post. Her sleeve. It was quite a tall post, and the fabric had been caught high up.

Well, at least it was something. But Maisie couldn't help feeling that her first—and only—clue made the whole mystery more confusing, not less . . .

"Maisie! There you are!"

Maisie stared at Gran in surprise. Why was she looking at her so strangely and fiddling with her apron strings like that? Perhaps she'd forgotten something? It was the middle of the morning, and Maisie was still feeling sleepy. She had just come in from fetching the vegetables from the greengrocer so Gran could cook the midday meal, and she had been quite quick about it, she was sure. “What’s the matter?” Maisie asked. “I’ve got the potatoes.”

Gran jerked her head toward the table, which was set with the best teacups and her silver teapot. And in the middle of the table was an envelope. A letter.

“It’s for you.”

Maisie recognized the scrawly writing even though she’d only ever had three letters penned in it—this would be the fourth. She had read the letters over and over, so that the paper was almost tearing where it had been folded and unfolded so many times.

It was from her father.

Maisie hadn’t seen him for two years, not since she was ten. He was the first mate on a steamship and he traveled around the world, carrying cargoes to and from all kinds of exotic places. *He would probably enjoy talking to the professor,* Maisie thought suddenly. *They must have been to some of the same countries.*

"Open it, Maisie," Gran begged. "What does he say?"

Maisie blinked. She had forgotten for a moment that as well as being her dad, he was Gran's son. Gran must miss him too. Carefully, she tore open the envelope and pulled out the letter, frowning as she tried to make out what it said. "He sends his love, and he saw dolphins. Um . . . and he's bought you an embroidered shawl for best. He'll bring it with him when he— Oh!"

"What? What? Is he ill?"

Maisie's hands trembled, and the letter shook. "He's coming home. He's going to retire from the sea, he says. At the end of his time on the *Lily Belle.* He's saved some money and he's going to go into business—selling ships' stores. He says he's written to you, too, to tell you all about it." She put the letter down on the table and stared at her gran. "The letter for you must still be on a ship somewhere. Or lost, maybe. He wrote this"—she checked the date—"weeks and weeks ago. Will he come back and live here?"

Gran slipped into the chair opposite her, dabbing at her eyes with her apron. "Yes, I should think so. Oh, my goodness!"

"He's never lived here that I remember," Maisie whispered. "He's always been at sea." She couldn't imagine seeing her father every day. Sitting opposite him to have breakfast. What if he wanted to move—somewhere closer to the docks, perhaps? What if he wanted Maisie to go with him?

She looked up at Gran, not sure what to say. Maisie could see how excited her grandmother was, how happy at the thought of her son coming home. And Maisie was too, of course she was. It would just be—different. That was all.

"Gran?" she murmured. "You haven't

minded looking after me all this time, have you?"

"Oh, of course not, Maisie." Gran reached across the table to squeeze Maisie's hand. "You know it's no hardship. Especially when you're such a help, leaving school to come and work in the house. But perhaps when your father returns and there's a little more money, you'll be able to go back to school."

Maisie swallowed. She couldn't imagine it—being a schoolgirl again. What about her detecting? She frowned down at the letter. What would her father think about that, anyway? She'd written to him, telling him about the cases she'd solved—the stolen money at the butcher's, the mystery at the theater, and her stay with Alice at the haunted house. But with the way it took letters so long to get overseas, and not even knowing where her father would be in port next, it was unlikely he'd had her letters yet. Sometimes it felt like she was sending letters to a ghost.

Maybe he wouldn't like the idea of his daughter being a detective. It was so long since she'd seen him, Maisie wasn't sure what he would think. She remembered him mostly as a person who always had a pocketful of mint humbugs, or licorice. And he had a beard, which was bristly and had reminded her of a nail brush.

"Such wonderful news." Gran sniffed again. "But he won't be back for a long while yet, Maisie. His voyage on the *Lily Belle* might still take a year, or even more. We mustn't be too excited."

Maisie nodded. Was she excited? She wasn't quite sure what she was feeling.

"Oh, there's the front door. Run and

answer it, Maisie dear. I'm not myself yet."

Maisie hurried upstairs as whoever it was kept ringing the bell and then started hammering on the door, too.

"Whatever is it?" Maisie gasped as she flung the door open. "Oh! Mr.— Er . . ." She had to try very hard not to call him Dinbers. "Mr. Danvers."

"I must see the professor at once! He sent me a telegram. The mask has been stolen! This is dreadful news. Absolutely dreadful. The pride of the collection!"

"Yes, sir." Maisie glanced up the stairs. She didn't think the professor would be particularly keen to see Mr. Danvers, but the man from the museum didn't look as though he'd be happy to wait in the hall. "Please come up, sir."

"Have the police been called?" Mr. Danvers snapped as he followed Maisie up the stairs.

"Yes, sir," Maisie told him, biting her lip to keep from saying that of course they had. The professor had gone to Scotland Yard in a cab first thing that morning, and brought the police back with him. They hadn't seemed particularly interested in the mystery, though, and the professor had been even more miserable after they left. He had told Maisie that the officer he spoke to hadn't really followed what he was talking about—the policeman couldn't understand how important the mask was, or how valuable. The professor had been reading the policeman's notes upside down. He was almost sure the officer had written down that a fancy-dress costume had been stolen.

"We shall have to offer a reward," Mr. Danvers was muttering. "I'll send a notice to all the newspapers. Ah, Professor! This is a catastrophe! How could it have happened?"

The professor rolled his eyes at Maisie, and drew Mr. Danvers inside. Maisie hovered on the landing, wondering if Mr. Danvers was serious about the newspapers. Gran would be furious.

The newspapers wouldn't print it, though, would they? Maisie thought hopefully. She would just not mention it to Gran . . .

"Look at that!" Gran shrieked, almost spilling her tea down the morning paper. "Oh, my goodness gracious. Look at it! It's practically a full page. And there's a drawing as well. I shall give the professor notice to leave. This has always been a respectable lodgings!"

Maisie leaned over to look at the paper. "It's not a very good drawing of the mask. I wonder if Mr. Danvers did it."

"As if it matters! Oh, Maisie, whatever are we going to do? There's a reward offered —five pounds, would you believe, for that worm-eaten old thing!"

"We'll have half of London turning up on our doorstep," Sally predicted, leaning over to look too.

“Don’t be cross with the professor, Gran,” Maisie pleaded. “This is all down to that Mr. Danvers from the museum. He said something about a reward.”

“That horrible, rude man! Typical.” Gran frowned, and then nodded. “Maisie, take the professor a cup of tea and some toast. He hardly ate any of his dinner last night, and he said he didn’t want breakfast, but he must have something, poor man.”

Maisie left Gran and Sally reading the newspaper article and muttering crossly to each other as she took the tea and toast upstairs. The professor was still in his dressing gown, looking gloomy. The men from the museum had come to take away the rest of the collection the day before, as planned, and his rooms seemed dreadfully empty without all the boxes and crates.

"Tea, sir." Maisie set the tray on a little table and glanced at the professor worriedly. His face was pale and he looked old. He had always been old, of course, but somehow he hadn't looked it before.

"Is there anything else you'd like— Oh!" Someone was banging at the door. "If it's that Mr. Danvers again . . ." Maisie sighed. "I'm sorry, Professor. I'd better go and answer it."

She dashed back down the stairs and opened the front door to a small boy, dwarfed by the huge box he was carrying. It was so big, he could hardly see around it, and his voice was muffled. "Delivery," Maisie thought he said, but that was all she caught.

"Thank you," she said, taking the box, which wasn't very heavy, and the boy sped off.

"He didn't say who it was for," Maisie murmured, balancing the box on the hall table and trying to find a label.

"Maisie!" The professor was hurrying down the stairs, his face transformed. "Someone has sent the mask back! Mr. Danvers was quite right to offer a reward after all."

"Oh!" Maisie looked doubtfully at the box. It was about the right size, she supposed. But surely if someone wanted the reward, he would bring the mask back himself so he could claim the money straightaway.

The professor pulled out his pocketknife and slit the string fastening the box, chortling happily to himself. As he lifted the lid away, Maisie peered inside, frowning.

The mask didn't look quite right.

There were feathers, certainly—but they were pink as well as red. And curled. And there were quite a lot of pink roses as well.

The professor reached in and hauled out a massive feathered hat, staring at it in horror.

"Oh dear . . ." he said. "Oh dear, Maisie, I suspect that this parcel was addressed to someone else. I just assumed . . ."

"It must be for Miss Lane," Maisie said, turning the box around to look. "A costume, maybe. Oh! It's addressed to Madame Lorimer." She looked up at the professor, and he stared at her in surprise. The elderly French lady wasn't the sort of person to wear an expensive, if rather horrible, feathery hat. "We'd better wrap it again and I'll take it up to her. I'm sorry, Professor."

"No, no, Maisie. I shouldn't have assumed it was the mask. It was silly of me." He trailed slowly back up the stairs. Maisie slid the hat back into the box and smiled to herself as she put the lid back on. Maybe Madame Lorimer had bought it because it reminded her of those pink iced buns with the coconut topping that she liked so much. Hopefully she wouldn't notice that the string had gone. Maisie carried the box up to her room and knocked.

"Entrez!"

Maisie was used to Madame Lorimer and knew that meant to come in. "Delivery for you, madame."

"Oh!" Surprisingly, Madame Lorimer flushed bright red and seized the box eagerly, pulling off the lid and beaming as she saw the hat inside.

"It's very pretty, Madame," Maisie told her —with her fingers crossed behind her back. Pretty if she wanted to go around looking like a walking meringue.

"Isn't it, Maisie?" Madame Lorimer put the hat on and admired herself in the mirror over the fireplace.

Maisie nibbled the back of her hand to stop herself giggling. She'd been wrong about the meringue. It was more like an

enormous, feathery pink mushroom . . .

"It's a present, Maisie," Madame Lorimer told Maisie, rather shyly. "From an . . . an admirer."

"Goodness!" Maisie stared at her.

"Yes. His name is Mr. Archibald Mossley. He wants me to marry him." She held out the little note that had been attached to the hat. "He says he can't wait to see me wearing it on our wedding day." She smiled. "Of course, the only sad thing is that when we are married, I shall be leaving you and your dear grandmother. I had been meaning to tell you."

Maisie nodded slowly. "Oh. Yes . . . Will it be soon?" Madame Lorimer had lived at 31 Albion Street for as long as Maisie could remember. She couldn't imagine the place without her. Maisie's earliest attempts at detection had been trying to work out where Madame had left her knitting.

"Oh, I won't be leaving for a few weeks yet. I will speak to your grandmother about it. I shall miss you all!"

"Yes . . . Us, too, Madame." Maisie wandered down the stairs as slowly and sadly as the professor had gone up them.

Everything was changing, it seemed. And not for the better. How could Madame Lorimer want to marry someone who bought her such a silly, horrible hat? Maisie slammed the door from the hallway as she went down toward the kitchen. Gran would tell her off, but she didn't care. Everything was strange, and new, and she didn't like it one bit.

And she still didn't have the slightest idea how to find the missing mask.

"No, that isn't the right one!" Maisie snapped. She wouldn't usually be so grumpy with someone who came to the door, but she was running out of patience. Sally had been right—half of London had seen the newspaper article, and the small, grubby boy standing on the front doorstep was the seventeenth person to try to claim the reward that morning. Maisie hadn't bothered the professor with any of the masks so far —she knew quite well what the real one looked like and she didn't want to get his hopes up again.

The little boy said that he'd found this one at the Underground station, but Maisie was quite sure he had made it himself.

"That's not the mask that's been stolen," she told him, through gritted teeth.

"Yes, it is!" he said stubbornly, holding out the mask for Maisie to get a better look. "Look, it's got feathers and everything! Just like in the picture!"

"It's made of paper! And it looks like you pulled those feathers out of a pigeon!" Maisie growled. "Or one of your mum's pillows, probably. I hope you get in trouble. Go away!"

The little boy stomped off down the front

steps, and Maisie could hear him making rude comments about her ginger hair as she stood in the doorway watching him go. It was amazing what people would do for the chance of five pounds. One man had actually turned up with a mask that was carved out of wood, just like the real one. Maisie had been taken in for a minute, until she realized that its eyes were the wrong shape. They were oval, the way that they had been drawn in the newspaper, but the real mask had eyes that were much squarer. It must have taken him hours to make, and he looked tired and hungry. She had felt bad turning him away. In fact, she had told him to go around to the back door and had given him a piece of meat pie that had been left in the larder.

She was just about to shut the front door again when she saw someone familiar—a man wrapped in layers of scarves, all topped off with a bowler hat. He was lurking just over the other side of the road. Maisie frowned, trying to remember where she had seen him before, but she couldn't quite place him. Then he turned slightly and she saw his long, droopy gray mustache. The image flashed into her mind at once—he had been hanging around outside the house on the day the mask was stolen.

Maisie gasped. Could he be the thief? Perhaps he had come back to see what other treasures he could steal! Maisie started down the steps, planning to race across the road and try to grab ahold of him—although she had no idea what she would do if she did actually manage to catch him. But then he had the cheek to cross over the road and walk toward the house.

Maisie ground her teeth. How dare he? He was even lifting his hat to her!

"Ah, good morning!"

"You've got a nerve," Maisie said furiously.

"I beg your pardon?" The elderly man froze, his hat held a little way above his bald head. He looked so surprised, and so altogether unlike a thief, that Maisie hesitated for a second.

But he had been hanging around outside the house. He *had.*

"You took it, didn't you?" she hissed at him. "I'll tell the police. The professor went to see them, you know! They're watching the house!" That wasn't true at all, but Maisie was too cross to care. How could he pretend to be so innocent?

"Miss, I assure you . . . there's been some mistake. My name is Archibald Mossley."

Maisie stopped, her mouth half open, and then swallowed. "Oh . . . Oh! Madame Lorimer's . . . um . . . gentleman friend."

He nodded politely, and Maisie felt her cheeks burn slowly red. She had just accused Madame Lorimer's fiancé of being a burglar.

"But—but—why were you hanging around the house the other day?" she muttered. "It was the day the professor's mask was stolen. I thought you had been looking for a chance to steal it . . ."

"Ah, yes. Dear Amelie mentioned this mask." It was his turn to go red. "It was nothing so dramatic, I'm sorry to say. I was—er . . ." He gave an embarrassed little cough. "I was coming to call on Madame Lorimer. I was trying to pluck up the courage to ring the doorbell. As I had—er, hmmm—something very important to ask her. That is—if she would do me the honor of becoming my wife."

"Oh . . ." Maisie nodded. Of course. It

made sense. He had only been hanging around outside because he was so nervous.

"I'm ever so sorry," she mumbled, her cheeks still pink with embarrassment. "And—um—congratulations, sir. It's just that you were there on the very day the mask was stolen. And there aren't really any other clues."

Mr. Mossley nodded sympathetically. "You were the young lady who was knocked down by the thief? Amelie told me about it. It must have been dreadful."

Maisie sighed. "The worst thing is I can't remember anything about it. If only I'd looked at his face! Or hers. I don't even know if it was a man or a woman," she added, remembering the little piece of fabric.

"Most upsetting," Mr. Mossley agreed, shaking his head.

"Would you like me to take you up to see

Madame Lorimer?" Maisie asked, opening the front door wider.

She escorted him up to the second floor, and then decided to go and check on the professor again. Perhaps she could tell him how she'd mistaken Mr. Mossley for the thief. It was quite funny, really, and it might cheer him up.

The professor was sitting at his desk, staring at the photo of himself and Daniel and the chief. He looked as if he had been sitting there for ages, and he hadn't eaten his toast, though he had managed the tea.

"I don't suppose you've remembered anything about that night, Maisie?" he asked hopefully as she slipped around the door.

Maisie sighed and shook her head. "I think I hit my head on the banister," she told him apologetically. "I can't really remember anything. Just that Eddie was barking and barking, and I thought I'd better go and see what was wrong. I *wish* I could remember! I'm sure I did see something, but I just can't pin it down."

The professor stared at her, his eyes narrowing, and Maisie looked back anxiously. Was he angry with her?

"What's the matter?" she said, biting her lip.

"Nothing, Maisie, just a thought . . ." He frowned. "It hadn't occurred to me before. Only when you mentioned pinning the memory down, it reminded me. Something we could try . . ."

"What?" Maisie hurried toward him and caught his hand. "Something that might help me remember? What do I have to do?"

"It's something I was shown when I visited India," the professor explained. "A way to clear your mind of all the clutter so that the important things shine through." He got up, fetching the straight-backed chair from in front of his desk. "Sit here, Maisie. Fold your hands in your lap and close your eyes. Now count your breaths."

Maisie opened one eye for a moment, not sure what he meant.

"Breathe in, counting to eight. Through your nose. Yes, like that. And now hold that breath for eight counts. And then breathe out through your mouth. And then the same again."

Maisie frowned, concentrating on the counting. She didn't feel as though she was going to remember anything. She was just worried about getting her numbers right.

"Gently. Slowly," the professor said, in a coaxing voice. "Is it getting easier?"

It was, Maisie decided, nodding slightly.

"And now, still with your eyes closed, try to look upward, to between your eyebrows. Try to feel the breath moving past that place . . ."

But it isn't, Maisie wanted to say. *It's nowhere near there!* She had a feeling, though, that she wasn't supposed to talk. So she did try, even though it didn't seem to make a lot of sense. And it was rather nice, just sitting still and breathing. She stopped worrying about her stupid mistake with Mr. Mossley, and how infuriating it was that she couldn't remember the night the mask was stolen.

The mask itself did keep popping into her head, though. Its odd, squarish eyes were floating around in front of the spot between her eyebrows, as though it was trying to tell her something. And then it bobbed away again, tucked under his arm.

His arm!

Maisie sat up with a screech. “I remember! Professor, I really do! It was like the mask came and told me—I *saw* it!”

“Ha. The information was there all the time. We just had to bring it out,” the professor said triumphantly. “Did you remember anything useful, Maisie?”

Maisie slumped back in the chair, frowning. “Well, I think so. But it seems a bit silly. It was definitely a man that I saw running off with the mask. He bumped into me by accident on the stairs, and I saw him just for a second, by candlelight. But, Professor—I think he was a *giant* . . .”

"Sausages. Joint of lamb. And the stewing steak. What does your gran want that for, Maisie? She doesn't usually have any stewing steak in the middle of the week." George, the butcher's boy, handed over the wrapped meat parcels from his bicycle basket, and looked curiously at Maisie. He was a little bit of a detective in his own way, Maisie thought. He knew all the customers' usual orders, and he always noticed if there was something different.

"It's for the professor," she told him. "He's so upset about the mask being stolen that he's not eating very much. Gran wants to make him some beef tea." Maisie made a face. "Rather him than me."

George looked confused. "I saw that story in the paper. But it said he was giving the mask to some museum, didn't it? Why's he so bothered about losing it if he was going to give it away anyway?"

Maisie frowned. "I know it's odd. But he wants other people to be able to see it, because it's so beautiful. And he really loved the people who gave it to him, I think. It was a thank-you gift—he rescued someone from an enormous snake!"

George wrinkled his nose. "Didn't look beautiful to me. Scary old thing." He glanced at her sideways. "You going to find it then, Little Miss Detective?"

"I wish I could. But I can't find where to start, George. All we've got is people turning up with fake masks all the time. No one knows anything about the real one." Maisie sighed. "For ages I couldn't remember anything about that night and who knocked me down. And now—well, I think the bump on the head might have sent me a bit silly. Don't laugh!"

George snorted. "Sent! As if you weren't already. Go on, what is it you've remembered?"

"A giant," Maisie said in a small voice.

But George was looking at her thoughtfully. He hadn't hooted with laughter the way she'd expected. "A giant . . . You never know, Maisie . . ."

"Not a fairy story, up-to-the-clouds sort of giant," Maisie added. "But really, really tall. As in, half as tall again as a normal person. I did wonder if there was a circus somewhere close by, but I haven't heard about one. You've not seen anything like that, have you?" she asked, not daring to hope.

"Might have done . . ." George nodded. "I do a delivery over at that old theater—the one on the other side of the park. You know where I mean?"

"But it's closed down," Maisie said.

"It *was,* but now it's been turned into a museum. Not like the museum that wants your professor's mask. This one's called Dacre's Museum of Curiosities. It's full of odd things. There's the most tattooed man in the world—Frank, one of the assistants at the butcher's shop, told me. And a mermaid, swimming in a great big glass tank. I thought I might go and see. Costs thruppence to go in, mind. It's a lot. Anyway, there's a giant on the posters they've got outside. And someone there's eating an awful lot of bacon and chops." He looked at her triumphantly.

Maisie squeaked and hugged him, which

was a shock for both of them. George nearly knocked his bike over.

"All right," he muttered. "Don't get excited."

"But it's a lead! It's definitely a lead, George."

"Could be," George agreed modestly. "Want to go and have a look around? After I've done my deliveries, of course."

"Yes, please." Maisie nodded seriously. She wanted to be a proper detective, and there was a bit of her that said it was feeble to get George to go with her. But all the rest of her said quite firmly that the giant had already knocked her down once and there was no point being *stupidly* brave. Besides, all detectives had faithful assistants. Usually she thought of Eddie as hers, but just for today she would have two of them.

George came back a couple of hours later, and Maisie and Eddie slipped quietly out into the yard. She was glad to go. The whole kitchen stank of the beef tea stewing on the stove. Even the dirty back streets smelled nicer, despite the horse droppings and piles of rubbish.

It was early afternoon, and fairly quiet. "Will it be open, this place?" Maisie asked as they hurried along, with Eddie scampering ahead. George had left his bike hidden behind the outhouse in the yard at Albion Street.

"Yup, I asked Frank, and he said it's open all afternoon and evening, but you pay more if you go for the proper shows in the evening—that's when the owner introduces all the curiosities, and they perform. But I don't reckon we need that. And besides, I haven't got sixpence for the evening show. It's still thruppence if you just want to go and have a look around, mind you."

Maisie nodded. Luckily, she did actually have enough. She still had the money from Mr. Lacey, and the professor had given her a whole shilling, as he said he felt dreadful that she'd been hurt trying to stop a burglar who was taking his mask. "I can pay for us both," she offered.

George sniffed proudly. "I can pay for myself," he told her, standing up a little straighter.

Maisie decided not to argue. "Is it a real mermaid?" she asked as they walked through the park, and she saw the old theater, its outside now decked in brightly colored banners and flags.

"Dunno." George shrugged. "Can't be, can it? No such thing . . . but Frank said it *looked* real."

"Hmm. Oh! I see the poster, with the giant." Maisie sped up. "That could be the person I saw . . . I don't remember his teeth being like that, though . . ."

The giant on the poster was wearing a leopard skin, and his top teeth were sharpened to points. His eyes were wild, and he looked as if he was growling.

George sniffed. "That's all for show, isn't it. I bet he isn't even that tall."

Maisie shivered. "He was big."

"Are you two coming in or not?" someone called, and Maisie jumped. She hadn't noticed that there was a little box outside the main doors, just big enough for a wizened old man in a gold-braided uniform. "Thruppence each," he said.

Maisie gulped. "Here you are." She

handed him her shilling, and George passed over three sticky pennies.

"Making my fortune, doing this," the old man grumbled. "All right then, here's your tickets, in you go." He handed them Maisie's change and two little slips of pasteboard, and waved at the heavy doors.

Maisie and George heaved them open, then tiptoed into the shadowy space of the foyer. It was nothing like the theater where Maisie had worked as a dresser for an actress friend of Miss Lane's a couple of months before. There the foyer had been glittering with mirrors and lights and flowers.

"They want it a bit dark," George said under his breath, "so you can't see too close. I bet half these curiosities are fake." He peered at another set of posters, these advertising a girl with wings. "Sewn on, I should think. Stuck to her dress."

"Let's go in anyway," Maisie whispered. The ghostly space was having an effect on her. She dreaded pushing open the next set of doors, which were made of heavy wood and very tall. They loomed up in front of her, dark and menacing.

But George didn't seem to be frightened —or at least he was very good at pretending that he wasn't. He shoved the doors open briskly and disappeared into the great dim space beyond. Maisie hurried after him, not wanting to be left alone. She didn't believe in ghosts and monsters and things like that, but the Museum of Curiosities was making the hair on the back of her neck stand up.

The theater auditorium was divided up with wooden partitions so that there were booths all around the outside, draped with velvety curtains and lit by flickering gas lamps. Strange figures loomed out of the light, and Maisie felt George's hand fumble for hers. Eddie was pressed tightly against her leg, a comforting warmth.

"This is spooky," George muttered. "Are you scared?"

"No . . ."

"Me neither." But he was holding her hand very tightly, Maisie noticed, and he jumped just as violently as she did when something whirled past them, skimming over their heads in a whoosh of wings.

"What was that?" Maisie yelped, and Eddie pressed closer against her, whimpering.

"A bird," George said. "Look." He pointed up to the top of one of the booths, where a strange hunched creature was now peering down at them.

"But it's got a face!" Maisie whispered. "It's a person. A girl! Like on the poster!"

"Don't be stupid. Flying people? That's even more silly than mermaids." But George sounded doubtful all the same.

It was a girl. She was sitting perched on the wooden wall, grinning down at them. Great feathery, leathery wings were folded

behind her, and her nails were like claws.

"This place is horrible," Maisie hissed. "Let's just find the giant." She pulled George after her around the line of booths, peering in at a bearded lady and the mermaid, who was in such a dark tank that it was impossible to tell if she was real or not. There was a swirling in the water, and a flick of tail—but that was all.

"Look!" George stopped short. "There he is. Blimey. He *is* big."

Maisie followed him slowly as he walked toward the booth. She had suddenly realized that the giant, if he really was the one who had broken in and taken the mask, might recognize her. The thought of being chased through this shadowy place by an angry giant was terrifying. She peered nervously around George at the massive figure, swathed in a sort of tunic and seated on a heavy wooden throne in the middle of the booth. *He must be at least seven feet tall,* she thought. But the huge man simply stared back at the children and winked. He took another bite of the massive bacon sandwich he was eating, and wiped his mouth on a tablecloth-size napkin. His teeth didn't look particularly sharp—just huge.

"Told you! I probably delivered that bacon," George pointed out rather proudly. "One giant, as promised. Think he's the one, Maisie?" he added in a whisper.

Maisie gulped and nodded. The professor's Indian memory technique had worked even better than she had realized. She recognized the crinkly blond hair, and the huge blue-green eyes, now that she saw him again. This bacon-eating person had

picked their front door lock, stolen from the professor, and knocked her down. But he looked perfectly pleasant, even if scarily big. “Yes. And look.” Turning away from the giant, she pulled the scrap of fabric out of her pocket, and George nodded, letting out a low whistle. It was proof. The pattern matched the ragged red and yellow tunic wrapped around the giant’s massive torso. *It is very tatty,* Maisie thought. *A bit could easily have torn off.*

“What do we do now?” George hissed. “I’m not going to ask him if he nicked a mask from your house. He might eat us alive! Did you see the size of his teeth?”

“I don’t really fancy asking him either,” Maisie murmured. “Let’s keep walking. I don’t understand why he’d steal the mask. He must have sold it to someone, I suppose . . .”

The next booth held "The World's Most Tattooed Man," according to the banner, but he was asleep, with a newspaper over most of him. They could see his legs, though, with a great ship sailing up one leg, and a sea monster wound around the other.

They headed on to a large booth in the corner of the theater, which was painted with a forest scene. The walls were covered in huge trees, dripping with vines, with an enormous spotted cat snarling from behind one of them. Sitting on a rock, which Maisie suspected was made of papier-mâché, was a bored-looking boy. He had skin the rich brown color of tea, and straight jet-black hair, and he was wearing nothing except a piece of fabric wrapped around his waist and some sort of feathery necklace around his neck.

No wonder he looks chilly, Maisie thought.

The boy saw them standing there, and rather sulkily he got up and drew a long, thin pipe from a sling across his shoulder. He put it to his lips and posed, ready to blow through the pipe at the painted cat.

"What's that, a pennywhistle?" George snorted.

"No . . ." Maisie breathed. "It's a blowpipe. For poison darts. Ones that make you fall down stiff as a board . . ." She looked at the sign above the booth. "'The Child of the Darkest Jungle.' Oh, I wonder . . . the Amazon jungle?"

She didn't think the boy could have heard her, but he lowered the pipe and turned to stare curiously into her eyes. Maisie gasped as the dim light fell full on his face.

It was the boy from the professor's photograph.

"All right, so tell it to me again . . ." George said, scowling. They were sitting on some iron steps in the alleyway that ran down the side of the theater, peering at each other in the gathering darkness. Maisie was trying to explain the professor's story to George, who said it was so far-fetched, it sounded like something out of a penny dreadful. Maisie wouldn't know—her gran wouldn't let her read those sorts of magazines.

"Just keep an ear out for anyone coming," Maisie reminded him. "The curiosities must go out sometime, for fresh air or to get some food. So, the professor saves the chief of the Amazon tribe from a huge snake, you see? And in return they give him the mask. And there's a photograph of the professor and the chief and the chief's grandson in the professor's room. It's that boy! Um . . . Daniel, the professor said he was called. I'm sure that's who he is! I recognized him. He had a necklace on, just like in the picture. He's a bit bigger now, but he would be, wouldn't he?"

"So you reckon he got his mate from the show to do the burgling?"

"Mmm. The lock was picked, we think. Maybe the giant knows how to do that . . ." Maisie frowned. It was hard to imagine the giant as a soft-footed cat burglar, but the burglary at the boarding house would have gone perfectly if it hadn't been for Eddie. Maisie glanced around, checking where the little dog was. He had been snuffling about looking for rats, but she hadn't seen him for a few minutes.

"Shhh! Someone's coming," Maisie whispered as the door began to open.

They drew back into the shadows of the

wall, but it was only the tattooed man. As he walked past they could see an extra eye painted in the middle of his forehead.

George gasped, suddenly sure that third eye could see him, and Maisie shivered. But the man hurried away down the alley.

George shook himself crossly, embarrassed to have shown Maisie he was scared. "What I don't get is why he'd want the mask back. Your professor said the tribe gave it to him. So what happened—they just changed their minds?"

"I don't know," Maisie said grimly. "That's what I'm going to try to find out. Where's Eddie? Can you see him?"

George looked down the alleyway. "Nope. Probably gone off to steal sausages from some poor lad."

"He only did that once!" Maisie said defensively. "Eddie! Eddie, where are you?"

Eddie suddenly bolted out from behind a pile of old wooden boxes, with his tail tucked between his legs and all the fur on his neck standing up. After him came a great gray rat, which was actually bigger than he was.

"Ugghh!" Maisie yelped, jumping up. "That's horrible! Eddie, here, it might bite you."

Eddie shot up the steps and hid behind Maisie, his whiskers quivering with a mixture of terror and excitement. The rat stopped at the bottom of the steps and eyed the three of them curiously. Then it turned around and walked slowly back to its den in the boxes. Maisie could have sworn it was swaggering.

"Look." George nudged her. "The door's opening again. Someone's coming." He hurried down the steps—staying as far away from the boxes as possible—and Maisie followed him. Eddie stayed safely halfway up the steps, still shivering.

The two children ducked behind the steps, where they could watch the door without being too obvious, and waited.

"It's him!" Maisie whispered.

"You sure?" George peered doubtfully at the figure. The light was going now, and it was hard to see.

"Yes, of course—he's just got clothes on, that's all. He couldn't go out in that little bit of cloth. He'd freeze." She jumped out from behind the steps and ran at the boy. "Hey!

What have you done with the mask?"

"Great," George muttered. "I'm glad we're not being obvious about it." But he stood behind her, trying to look fierce.

The boy glared back at Maisie and pulled something out of his sleeve like a conjuring

trick. It was a long wooden pipe, which he raised to his lips.

His dark eyes fastened on Maisie's as he puffed out his cheeks, ready to blow.

"Maisie, get down!" George yelled, pulling Maisie's arm. "He's got those poison dart things."

Maisie stumbled sideways, staring in horror at the boy, at his glinting eyes and puffed cheeks. She wondered what sort of poison was on the feathered dart he had tucked into the end of the blowpipe. The professor had said that some tribes made poison out of roasted frogs . . .

Then, from out of the corner of her eye, Maisie saw a little white and brown ball leap into the air, and the boy let out a shout of surprise as the blowpipe was snatched out of his hand. Eddie trotted back to Maisie and spat it out at her feet, wagging his tail proudly. Then he turned around, sat down in front of her, and glared hard at the boy.

"G-good dog," Maisie said. "Good boy, Eddie."

The boy looked down at his hand as though he didn't quite understand how the blowpipe wasn't in it anymore, and then he sighed.

"Can I have it back, please?" he asked, in clear, slightly accented English.

"Are you joking?" George demanded. "You were going to shoot us! With poison darts!"

"No, I was not." He shrugged. "They are not poisoned. It is just for the show. I only wanted you to leave me alone. Look." He pulled a tiny, feather-topped sliver of wood out of his pocket, and pricked the tip of his thumb. "There. See?"

"Oh . . ." Maisie let out a deep sigh of relief.

"But I will not give you the mask," the boy added.

"Please! You have to, Daniel." Maisie gazed at him, pleadingly. "My friend Professor Tobin is so upset that it's gone. You know him! He told me about you. He was the one who taught you to speak English. You can't want to hurt him."

"I do not." Daniel shook his head. "But I cannot give the mask to him. I have to take it back home with me."

"Why?" George demanded. "I thought it was your granddad who gave him the mask in the first place. Suddenly he wants it back?"

"Yes."

Maisie and George stared at him, and Daniel sighed. "The mask is very old, and it's been worn by many of our tribe. We wear it for the dances—when we honor the trees, and the animals we hunt. But then my granddad gave the mask to the professor, to honor *him,* you see. He was very brave, rescuing my granddad from the snake."

Maisie nodded, smiling proudly.

"But in the time since the professor left and the mask went with him, our tribe has had bad luck. My brother and sister are very sick. And two of my cousins were killed by a black jaguar when they were hunting. Our tribe met together and decided that we should not have given away the mask. So I was sent to bring it back, because the professor had taught me your language."

Maisie frowned. "But it's such a long journey!"

Daniel shrugged. "I know. I have been many months away from my home."

"What are you doing here then?" George demanded. "In the show?"

"I ran out of things to trade," Daniel explained. "I had some furs, but that was all. And the boat passage was very costly. By the time I arrived here, I had nothing. Albert —the giant, you know—he found me at the docks. I was very hungry, and he gave me food and told me he had somewhere I could stay. He used to work on a ship as a boy, before he grew too tall. He was visiting an old shipmate on the *Invincible.* So for the last two months I've been performing here. When I could get out, I searched for the mask. But Mr. Dacre, he does not like me to leave the theater in case I run away."

He ducked his head, his cheeks reddening. "I did not know how big a city this was, and how difficult it would be to find the mask. I did not know what to do. My people had sent me on this sacred journey. How could I go back and tell them I had failed?"

Maisie nodded. "Let me guess. Then you saw the articles in the newspaper about the professor giving his treasures to the museum."

"There was a photograph of the professor with the mask, Albert showed it to me. And then I recognized Professor Tobin's name when Albert read me the story. I cannot read English. I can only speak it."

"Your English is very good. The professor must have taught you a lot," Maisie said.

"I had practice on the ship as well," Daniel agreed solemnly. "The sailors talked to me. And since I have been here, I listen to all the things people say."

"What I don't understand," Maisie said thoughtfully, sitting down on the iron staircase again, "is why you didn't just go to the professor and explain about all your relatives being sick and getting eaten by jaguars. I bet he would have just given you the mask! He would have been so happy to see you again."

Daniel shook his head. "But no! The mask was to go to a museum, the newspaper said. A place like this, where people would come and stare at it, and point, and throw things." He shuddered. "I could not let that happen.

It would be wrong. And it made me sad that the professor would give the mask to that sort of place. He must not understand how special it is."

"People throw things at you?" Maisie whispered.

"All the time," Daniel told her grimly. "Peanuts. Rotten fruit. Do you not see? I had to take the mask back."

Maisie frowned. She could see that the boy was upset, but from the way the professor had talked about the British Museum, people certainly wouldn't be allowed to throw *anything.* Then she understood. The Museum of Curiosities—it was the only museum Daniel had ever seen. Of course he thought that the mask would be going somewhere just as horrible.

"The museum that the mask was going

to isn't like this one," she tried to explain. "It's huge, the professor told me. He's going to take me there one day. It has all sorts of beautiful things in it, very special and important things. Not—well—monsters. I don't mean you're a monster," she added hurriedly. "But this is a show—the British Museum is different . . ." She could see that Daniel didn't really believe her, though, and she could understand why.

"Did you pick the lock?" George asked suddenly.

"Albert did," Daniel explained. "He said you learn all sorts of things in a place like this. A conjuror taught him how to do it, years ago. And Albert took the mask for me too. I felt wrong, creeping into the house and stealing it. The mask is too special, you see . . ." He glanced worriedly at Maisie.

"Albert was very sorry that he knocked you down. He did not mean to hurt you."

Maisie nodded. "It's all right."

George gave a disapproving snort. "Her gran was really worried about her," he told the boy. "And anyway, what are you still doing here? Shouldn't you be off back to your jungle with the mask?"

"I have no money for the ship." Daniel hung his head. "Mr. Dacre will not give it to me. He says I owe it to him for my food and these clothes."

"That isn't fair!" Maisie cried. "Listen, I promise that the professor loves the mask, almost as much as you do. If you explain, I'm sure he'll say you should keep it. And I think he might be able to help you get back home."

George scowled. "He's a thief!" he

said under his breath, but Maisie elbowed him. "You were accused of stealing once, remember?"

Daniel stared at her with a little hopeful frown. "I will fetch the mask," he suggested. "To show the professor that it is safe." He glanced nervously back at the door. "I must be quick—Mr. Dacre will be coming to start the evening show. Shall I get it now?"

"Yes!" Maisie nodded, and Daniel vanished back into the theater.

It was very odd, Maisie thought as she sat on the steps, patting Eddie and trying to ignore George's disapproving look. She had solved the mystery. But everything was still so complicated . . .

Maisie and George hurried back to Albion Street with Daniel between them, the mask in his arms, wrapped up in a piece of cloth.

"You are sure that the professor will not be angry?" Daniel murmured as they arrived at the boarding house.

"I don't think he will be angry at all," Maisie assured him. "I think he'll be so happy to see you. He told me that he wished he could have brought you back to England with him before. I'm sure he'll want to help you get home," she added, crossing her fingers hopefully behind her back. "Unless you decide to send the mask home, and stay here."

Daniel shook his head. "No, I like my own home—here everything is too crowded. Too busy."

"Huh," George sniffed. "At least we don't get eaten by jaguars."

Maisie led them both across the yard to the back door. Gran and Sally would be busy preparing the evening meal—extra busy, as Maisie wasn't there to help.

"And just where have you been, miss?" Gran asked as they came in. She was bent over the stove, stirring ferociously at pans,

and she didn't see who Maisie had with her.

"Goodness gracious!" Sally gasped, staring at the boy, and Gran turned around, peering through the steam.

Maisie could see why they were surprised. Daniel did seem very out of place in the kitchen, with his red-brown skin and jet-black

hair. Even though he was wearing perfectly normal trousers and a worn jacket over a grubby shirt, he still looked most unusual.

"Who on earth are you?" Gran snapped.

"He's brought the professor's mask back, Gran," Maisie explained. "George helped me find him."

"Told you where to find him, more like," George muttered. "Er, evening, Mrs. Hitchins," he added hastily, whipping off his flat cap.

"So, please, can we just go and tell the professor?" Maisie begged. "Then I'll come down and help with the dinner."

"You've found it? This mask that he's been fussing about?"

"Yes, Gran."

"For heaven's sake, Maisie, take it to him at once! It's more than I can stand, having him moping round the house. He looks like he's been slapped in the face with a wet fish. I can't be doing with it."

"Yes, Gran!" Maisie dashed upstairs with George and Eddie and Daniel following her, and knocked loudly on the door of the professor's rooms.

"Hello?" Even through the door, the professor sounded downhearted.

Maisie flung it open and pushed the boy in front of her. "Professor, look who we've found!"

"Daniel!" The professor jumped out of his armchair as though he had seen a ghost, and the boy stared back at him guiltily. "It's so wonderful to see you—but what are you doing in London? However did you get here?" Then he frowned a little—he was a very, very clever man, after all, and it didn't take him long to work things out. "Daniel, did you come all this way for the mask?"

Daniel nodded. "The hunting was so bad —we didn't have enough food. Then the black jaguar killed my cousins when they were out after monkeys. And little Pachiri and Tuia are very ill. They were when I left, I mean. By now . . ." He shrugged sadly.

"But this is dreadful!" The professor caught his hands, pressing them worriedly. "My poor boy!"

"It was the mask! We should never have given it away, Professor. The spirits did not like it. I was coming to ask if we could have it back, but I did not know how to find you. And then I saw that you were giving it to a museum. This girl, she says it is a good place, but I did not understand. So—I took it."

Daniel held out the mask, pulling away

the cloth wrapping so that the face shone out in the dim room, surrounded by the blazing feathers.

George stepped back, shuddering, and even Maisie, who had seen it so many times before, let out a little gasp. Seeing it like that, suddenly it was easy to believe that the spirits of the forest were looking through those gaping eyes. She could see why Daniel's people were so desperate to have it back.

The professor sighed happily and ran a loving hand down the side of the feathers. Maisie was almost sure the mask's face changed as he did it, so that it was smiling.

"I'm so sorry, Daniel. I never meant to carry away something so special. And I hadn't realized it would be wrong to send it to a museum. How stupid of me. Of course you must take it home with you."

"Professor, the tribe didn't have money to send him here . . ." Maisie said, trying to be tactful. "They sent him with goods to trade, but not enough. Daniel's been working at a . . . a show to earn enough money to live on. It's a horrible place."

"Goodness. We must make sure that your passage home is organized, and on a good ship, with a trustworthy crew." The professor nodded firmly. "I shall see to it tomorrow morning, first thing." He bustled around the room, digging into corners. "I'm sure I have another of those boxes somewhere, or perhaps a strong canvas carrying bag. You won't want it to go in the hold, will you?"

Maisie and George grinned at each other in relief, and Maisie perched herself on the arm of a chair with a little sigh. Now that everything was organized, she felt so tired.

It was then that they heard a furious banging on the front door.

Maisie jumped up with a squeak. "Oh! I'd better go and answer it. Gran and Sally are busy with the dinner."

She ran down the stairs, wondering who on earth it could be. "I'm getting it, Gran!" she called. "I'm just coming, stop banging like that!"

She flung the door open and glared at the three men on the front steps. "You didn't have to break the door down . . ." Then her voice trailed off as she realized that the men at the door had black uniforms on, shining with silver buttons, and tall hats.

Just at the worst possible time, the police had arrived.

"Er, yes?" Maisie asked politely.

"Excuse me, miss, but one of our plainclothesmen has been keeping watch on the house . . ." the oldest of the policemen said. He had a lot more silver braid around the sleeves of his tunic, and Maisie reckoned he was probably an inspector.

"*Has* he?" Maisie asked, feeling shocked. Why on earth hadn't she seen him? Still, she had been quite occupied, what with all the fake mask people and worrying about the professor.

"Yes, miss. At the request of Mr. Danvers, from the museum. He thought that the thief might try to return for more of the professor's collection. So he asked for someone to be on watch."

"Oh . . ." Maisie swallowed nervously.

Had they seen her and George bringing Daniel back? Did they think he was suspicious?

"And, er, is there a problem?" she asked.

"We've had ever so many people coming with fake masks, trying to claim the reward. It's quite a nuisance."

"Yes, miss. But the plainclothes officer

reported in a few minutes ago, saying that he'd seen a young boy of foreign appearance with a parcel, miss. Mr. Danvers was of the opinion that the mask was in the parcel. He happened to be at the Yard—er—visiting. He's very interested in the case." The policeman coughed politely, and one of the others smirked.

Maisie had a suspicion that Mr. Danvers had been at Scotland Yard rather a lot.

"Mr. Danvers is on his way now . . ." The policeman glanced down the street. "Would we be able to come in, miss, and speak to the professor? My name is Inspector Morris, if you could tell him."

Maisie nodded. She was desperately trying to think. She couldn't let the police go upstairs and find the mask, and Daniel.

Mr. Danvers wanted that mask. A lot.

What had he called it? The pride of the collection? He was never going to agree that it should go back to the Amazon with Daniel, even though it was really up to the professor whom he gave it to. And now the police were involved as well, and the theft of the mask had been reported as a crime. They would probably decide to put Daniel in prison, whether the professor wanted him arrested or not.

Maisie was fairly sure that being in prison would be even more awful for Daniel than it would be for anybody else, as he was such a person of the outdoors and the forest. And he was only a little older than she was. Even if the professor managed to get him out quickly, it would still be terrible. She couldn't let it happen, she decided. She stepped back into the hallway, opening the door wider

and beckoning the policemen in after her.

"I'm ever so sorry, sir," she explained politely to Inspector Morris, turning a little so that she was facing more toward the stairs, and raising her voice. She was quite sure she had left the door to the professor's rooms open when she came down to answer the door. She hoped so, anyway. "But I'm afraid Mr. Danvers is quite wrong. The boy—his name is Daniel—is an old acquaintance of the professor's, from his travels in the Amazon, you know. He's living in London now and performing at Dacre's Museum of Curiosities. I went to visit the museum today with one of my friends, and happened to meet him, so I told him that the mask had been stolen. He was very sorry to hear it, so he decided to give another mask to the professor, one that he had brought with him from the Amazon."

Maisie paused for breath, hoping that the professor and Daniel and George had heard all this from upstairs. If they had any sense, they would hide the feathered mask and get out the rather battered one with the ratty fur trim that the professor had decided the museum didn't need. They could pretend Daniel had brought that one around. She hoped the inspector couldn't tell she was making all this up. He had very bright eyes and foxy-colored hair, and he looked decidedly too clever.

"How kind of him," the inspector replied, just as politely. "Perhaps we could see it? And Mr. Danvers as well, when he arrives?"

Maisie gulped and tried to smile. "Of course. I'll show you up."

She led the procession of policemen

slowly up the stairs, her crossed fingers hidden in the folds of her skirt, and then knocked at the half-open door to Professor Tobin's rooms.

"Good afternoon, sir. Some policemen to see you."

The professor, who was showing George and Daniel something in a book, looked up in surprise. Pretend surprise, Maisie realized in relief. The battered fur-trimmed mask was lying on his desk, and there was no sign of the feathered one at all.

"Ah! Wonderful! Is there some news of my mask?" the professor asked hopefully. He really was a very good actor, Maisie thought.

"I'm afraid not, sir." Inspector Morris stared at him thoughtfully. "As I was explaining to this young lady, our plainclothes officer saw a young boy arriving, with what could have been the mask. Mr. Danvers is convinced that the mask has been returned, by the thief." Here he glanced at Daniel, who was staring at him in horror. "Although he couldn't explain why . . ." Inspector Morris glanced out of the professor's window and sighed. "Here he is now, I'm afraid. Perhaps one of my constables could let him in?"

One of the younger policemen went off downstairs, and as soon as he opened the front door, everyone could hear Mr. Danvers ranting about the mask and the shameless thief. "It's quite obvious! The thief's brought it back to try to claim the reward!" he shouted as he came dashing up the stairs.

"No one would be that stupid," Maisie muttered, and saw Inspector Morris looking at her curiously. She shuffled over to George and breathed, "Where's the mask?" into his ear.

"Hidden in that old blanket chest on the landing," George whispered back. "I crept out and did it when we heard you talking."

Maisie tried hard to keep a relieved smile off her face as Mr. Danvers burst into the room. Eddie growled at him, which just showed what sort of horrible person he was.

"Where is it? Where is it? Get away, you dratted creature!"

The professor looked at him with a confused frown. "I'm so sorry, my dear fellow, I don't quite understand. Daniel here has been kind enough to bring me a replacement mask, that's all. The feathered mask is still missing."

Mr. Danvers was practically spitting with rage. "Stuff and nonsense! Codswallop! This is the thief, it must be! Arrest that boy at once!"

"Sir, we have no proof," Inspector Morris

said firmly. "Of course, we may have our suspicions." He looked thoughtfully from Maisie to Daniel, and then to George, who was doing his best impression of a stupid delivery boy who had no idea what was going on. "Things may not be quite as they seem. But there is no feathered mask here."

"They've hidden it!" Mr. Danvers gibbered. "It's that girl! She's a nasty piece of work. You should arrest her, too."

Maisie gasped, and the professor marched into the middle of the room, scowling fiercely. "This is absolutely inexcusable! Miss Hitchins is the granddaughter of my landlady and her family are of excellent character. How dare you make such accusations? I should like you to leave at once, sir, before I reconsider my very generous gift to your museum!"

Mr. Danvers stared at him, his face quite white with anger except for two burning red spots across his cheekbones. Then he snarled, "Codswallop!" again, and marched out of the room.

"My apologies . . ." Inspector Morris said. "We will, of course, keep up the very careful watch on the house, just in case the burglar returns." And he followed Mr. Danvers out.

Maisie stared at the others in dismay, then ran to shut the door after the police. When she got back to the professor's rooms, he was slumped in his armchair, exhausted. Daniel and George were staring out the window.

"Yeah, I reckon it's him over there." George pointed across the street. "With the cap on. He's just hanging around. Can't believe I didn't spot him before. Look, he's still got his regulation boots on!"

"And they're watching the yard, too," Maisie said dismally. "They must have been, if they saw us coming in that way. We'll never get the mask out without them seeing."

"I s'pose you could just wait a while," George suggested, looking at Daniel. "Give it a couple of months—they won't keep a rozzer watching the house that long."

"I wouldn't put it past that inspector to come back and search again," the professor said worriedly. "I don't think he was quite convinced by our little act."

Daniel nodded miserably. "But I have no choice. We cannot take the mask away. Maisie is right. And yet the longer I wait, there are more disasters happening to my family."

Maisie chewed her lip. She didn't really believe that giving the mask away had brought bad luck to Daniel's tribe, but it was clear that *he* did. And he was desperate to get home. If he went back to the Museum of Curiosities now, he would be in terrible trouble for being away so long. And it was such an awful place. She didn't want him to have to stay there a moment longer.

She agreed with the professor, too. The inspector had looked worryingly sharp-eyed. But there was just no way they could get the mask out of the house, back or front. She glared out the window at the police officer in disguise.

Unless . . .

Unless the mask was disguised too, somehow.

It would be very hard to hide something that big, and covered in bright red feathers, though. It didn't really look like anything else.

Suddenly Maisie gasped. "George! Get the mask out of the blanket chest. I've got an idea!" She dashed off up the next flight of stairs. It was after tea, but before dinner, which meant that Madame Lorimer would almost certainly be dozing on her sofa.

Maisie crept into her sitting room and

seized the feathery pink and red mushroom of a hat. She glanced guiltily over at Madame Lorimer, snoring delicately by the window, and promised herself that she would bring the hat back in a few minutes. Then, frowning to herself, she borrowed Madame's paisley shawl from the hook on the back of the door too.

"Look!" she exclaimed as she burst back into the room. "We can hide the mask in here!"

The professor and the two boys looked at her doubtfully. "Is that a hat?" George asked at last.

"Yes," Maisie sighed. "I know. Madame Lorimer's gentleman friend gave it to her. But look, the feathers are almost the same color. If we just fluff it up a bit . . ." She lifted up a swath of pink net and slipped the mask underneath, so that only the red feathers billowed out.

"It looks dreadful," the professor said, rather apologetically. "But it did before. Does Madame Lorimer actually wear the thing?"

"She wore it to walk in the park yesterday," Maisie said, wrapping the paisley shawl around herself and carefully lifting the hat onto her head.

"You look like an explosion in the Regent's Park Zoo," George snorted, and even Daniel was sniggering.

"Fine," Maisie snapped. "Laugh all you like. But it'll work. It will, won't it?" she asked the professor.

He nodded. "No one would try to sneak stolen goods out in something so—so—er, eye-catching. I think you will be quite safe, Maisie."

"All right." George shrugged. "You go on out the front dressed like that, and I'll fetch my bike from the yard. I'll meet you in the park, and you can put the mask in my basket. I'll hide it at my place till the professor has got Daniel's passage booked for the Americas. Then I'll bring it to the docks. Oi, watch it!" he snapped as Maisie hugged him. "That thing could smother me! I'm off to fetch the bike."

The professor nodded. "We are very grateful, George, believe me." He dug half a sovereign out of his waistcoat pocket, and George's eyes went as round as saucers. "Much obliged!" George stammered, and raced off down the stairs.

"You can rest here for a few days," the professor added to Daniel. "I can't bear the thought of you in that dreadful show. I'll speak to your grandmother, Maisie, though I suspect she won't be pleased . . ."

Maisie wrapped the shawl tighter around her shoulders. "Eddie, stay here with the professor," she murmured. "They'll never believe I'm Madame Lorimer if I've got you with me."

Eddie whined, but the professor fed him a biscuit from the tin on his desk, and the dog disappeared under the armchair to gobble it up.

Maisie tiptoed down the stairs, trying to

walk as though her feet hurt, like Madame Lorimer with her corns. At the bottom she glanced back and saw Daniel and the professor watching her anxiously.

Maisie let herself out of the front door and pattered down the steps, trying hard not to glance at the plainclothes police officer, who was loitering by the lamppost on the other side of the road. She tried not to look worried, but she was sure she could feel eyes fixed on her. *It's just the hat,* she told herself firmly. *Of course everyone's looking.* A little girl pointed at her as she walked past, and her mother told her off.

"Oi!" a voice thundered behind her, and Maisie drew up the trailing shawl, ready to run. She had been spotted! She glanced back in horror—but the police officer was roaring at a little boy who had bowled a hoop into the man's legs and was now running off in terror. Maisie pressed a hand to her

thumping heart, and carried on walking.

She reached the end of the road, with no thudding of footsteps behind her and no police whistle. Maisie risked a tiny glance back as she rounded the corner. The police officer was leaning against the lamppost now, looking bored. They had done it!

"Goodbye! Goodbye! Stay away from those big snakes!" Maisie called up from the quayside, waving her hat, and Eddie yelped happily. He had grown very fond of the boy during the few days he had stayed with the professor. Daniel was very generous with the professor's biscuits.

"Remember me to your granddad!" Professor Tobin called. "And keep looking

at that book!" He had been trying to teach Daniel the basics of reading, and had sent Maisie out to a bookshop for a child's primer.

The professor was very proud of Daniel's progress. Maisie suspected that he still hoped the boy would come back one day, although from Daniel's expression it looked like he couldn't wait to return to the jungle.

"It's going—look, they're casting off all the ropes," Maisie cried, jumping up and down. There was something incredibly exciting about seeing such a huge ship move off on its voyage, even if she wasn't traveling herself. Perhaps one day she would, though. Maybe her father would take her on a ship, once he was back. Maybe she would even travel abroad to solve a mystery, like her hero, Gilbert Carrington.

"Don't fall in!" George cried. "Honestly, Maisie Hitchins, I'm not jumping in after you! Ah, look, they're off!"

"Oh, I can't see Daniel!" Maisie said sadly as the ship began to pull away.

"Here, missie," came a deep voice from beside her. Albert the giant had come to say goodbye to his friend too. "You come up here with me and wave the little lad off." The giant stooped down and scooped Maisie up onto his shoulder. "There, better now?"

"Yes, thank you." Maisie gulped, gripping his arm tightly. The view was much, much better. She could see Daniel properly now, waving and beaming at her.

Maisie waved and waved until the ship was toy-size and they couldn't

see Daniel standing by the rail any longer.

The feathered mask was on its way home.

The Case of the Stolen Sixpence

When Maisie rescues an abandoned puppy, he quickly leads her to her first case. George, the butcher's boy, has been sacked for stealing, but Maisie's sure he's innocent. It's time for Maisie to put her detective skills to the test as she follows the trail of the missing money . . .

The Case of the Vanishing Emerald

When star-of-the-stage Lila Massey comes to visit, Maisie senses a mystery. Lila is distraught —her fiancé has given her a priceless emerald necklace, and now it's gone missing. Maisie sets out to investigate, but nothing is what it seems in the theatrical world of make-believe . . .

The Case of the Phantom Cat

Maisie has been invited to the country as a companion for her best friend, Alice. But as soon as the girls arrive, they are warned that the manor house they're staying in is haunted. With Alice terrified by the strange goings-on, it's up to Maisie to prove there's no such thing as ghosts . . .

The Case of the Secret Tunnel

Gran's new lodger, Fred Grange, says he works for a biscuit company, but Maisie has noticed him coming and going at odd hours, and he seems to know nothing about biscuits! While trying to uncover the truth about Mr. Grange, Maisie is drawn into a mystery that takes her deep underground . . .

Find out more about Holly Webb